I CAN FLY

BY RUTH KRAUSS
ILLUSTRATED BY JAN BRETT

GOLDEN PRESS • NEW YORK
Western Publishing Company, Inc., Racine, Wisconsin

 Library of Congress Catalog Card Number: 80-83422 ISBN 0-307-10111-8/ISBN 0-307-68111-4 (lib. bdg.) G H I J

A BIRD can fly.
So can I.

A cow can moo.
I can too.

I can grab like a crab.

I can squirm like a worm.

Pick pick pick
I'm a little chick.

Who's busy like a bee?
Me me me.

Who can climb anywhere?
Me! Like a bear.

My house is
like a mouse's.

A clam is what I am.

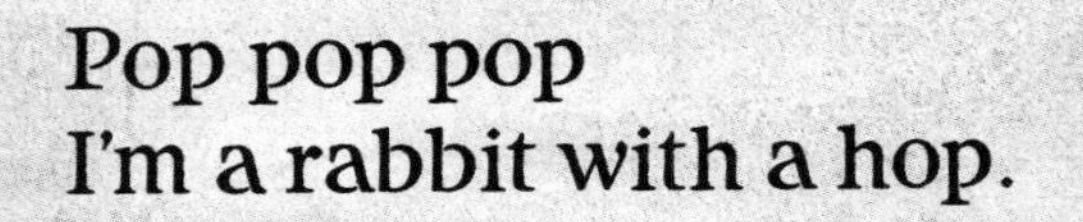

Pop pop pop
I'm a rabbit with a hop.

Bump bump bump
I'm a camel with a hump.

Howl howl howl
I'm a wild screech owl.

Gubble gubble gubble
I'm a mubble in a pubble.

I can play
I'm anything that's anything.
That's my way.